Fallout

Fallout

Nikki Tate

With Best Wishes
Nikki Tate
2011.

orca soundings

ORCA BOOK PUBLISHERS

Library and Archives Canada Cataloguing in Publication

Tate, Nikki, 1962-
Fallout / Nikki Tate.
(Orca soundings)

Issued also in electronic format.
ISBN 978-1-55469-976-6 (bound).--ISBN 978-1-55469-272-9 (pbk.)

I. Title. II. Series: Orca soundings
PS8589.A8735F34 2011   JC813'.54   C2009-906877-X

First published in the United States, 2011
Library of Congress Control Number: 2011929242

Summary: After the death of her sister, Tara struggles to deal with her guilt
through slam poetry.

*Orca Book Publishers is dedicated to preserving the environment and has printed
this book on paper certified by the Forest Stewardship Council®.*

Orca Book Publishers gratefully acknowledges the support for its publishing
programs provided by the following agencies: the Government of Canada
through the Canada Book Fund and the Canada Council for the Arts,
and the Province of British Columbia through the BC Arts Council
and the Book Publishing Tax Credit.

Cover photography by dreamstime.com

ORCA BOOK PUBLISHERS
PO Box 5626, Stn. B
Victoria, BC Canada
V8R 6S4

ORCA BOOK PUBLISHERS
PO Box 468
Custer, WA USA
98240-0468

www.orcabook.com
Printed and bound in Canada.

14 13 12 11 • 4 3 2 1

*For those who stepped back from the edge
and turned to the future.*

Rain bashes lilies
left at her headstone
smashes petals
leaves them ugly, forlorn.

Didn't she know
how flowers melt into accusations
how they paint ragged smears
over granite
over grass
over graves?

Chapter One

My sister, Hannah, bought a bottle of vodka from some guy she met outside the liquor store. I doubt Hannah knew his name. She probably didn't care. Hannah, by that point, didn't care about much.

She was fifteen, which is why she needed this guy to buy the booze. Maybe he felt sorry for the girl with the crutches. Maybe he thought a drink would make her feel better. Maybe she paid him.

The police found the bottle. It was half empty and still inside a brown paper bag. What's amazing is the bottle wasn't broken. Not like Hannah. A kid with crutches is no match for the front end of a bus.

What was she thinking before she took that last step? Did she think about me? Mom and Dad? Did she wonder if it would hurt? Did she think about the mess she would leave behind? Or did she just take a deep breath and step out into traffic?

My sister took a lot of secrets to her grave.

I wasn't there when Hannah stepped in front of the bus. In my nightmares, though, I stand behind her on the curb. Then, I push her.

The bus brakes squeal. I scream, "Stop!"

Every dream ends with me on a stage. I am naked. All I have to protect me is my poetry. I yell poem after poem at the audience, trying to make them understand.

I killed my sister.

She won't let me forget.

Chapter Two

"Put your hands together for Tara Manson!"

I step into the spotlight. The audience is out there, though I can't see them.

This moment is mine. I can say anything in my poems.

Have you ever faced fear
and jumped

4

into churning waters
So deep there is no bottom?

I have. At the waterslides.

There's always a chuckle after I say
that line. Maybe I look too heavy to be
a waterslide type. Whatever. It's my job
to deliver the poem. The audience hears
what they want to hear.

I change my voice so I sound like
I'm in a commercial.

Splash Kingdom!
Your fun in the sun
place to plunge
in and away from
what really matters.

Then I go back to my normal voice.

So what
if the phone ringing

in your beach bag
needs to be answered.

Here, I point at the audience.

No. You don't get it.
Not like a hey, hi, how's it going?
    see you later, whatever
kind of call
but a message you need to get now
not tomorrow
not some other time
but right this second or
someone will die.

Then I start again, softly.

When fun calls
it's wrong to ignore
sun and sweat
skin on skin
his lips on mine

my lips drinking him in
this wild ride down
slippery when wet
curves ahead.
Fun is all good, right?

Here's where I speed up and get
louder.

THIS is all that matters
because we only live once
and all that living
is churned and pushed into
one glorious afternoon at the
*   waterslides.*

You hear what I'm saying?

How can they hear what I'm saying?
I can speak fast and loud, but they can't
really know what it was like that day
last summer. One year ago—today.

The whole, long, sun-baked day David
and I played, splashed, laughed…while
Hannah was—

The sound of fingers clicking moves
through the audience. They think I've
lost my place. This is their way of telling
me to keep going.

Plunge feet first
Down Big Mountain
Time Tunnel
Jumbo Splash
Race and giggle
catch each other
and sprint to the snack stand
hot dogs and plastic cheese.

I ignore the ringing phone, for once.
Turn my back on her, for once.
Snap it shut. Click it off, for once.
Toss it under a damp towel
and forget

that outside this moment
in my heat-soaked day
a tragedy unfolds
one phone call away.

The applause washes over me. I dip in a modest bow.

Rick, the host, shakes my hand. "Careful going down the steps," he says. "Judges, let's see your scores for Miss Tara…"

He calls them out. The low score is a 7.1 and the high an 8.9. That should be enough to get me through to the second round of the poetry slam.

When I touch my fingertip to my cheek, it's wet. When I touch my fingertip to my tongue, I taste salt.

Chapter Three

Outside the Koffie Klub it's muggy. I'm still not used to this humid Ontario summer weather. On the west coast it cools off at night. Not here in Camden.

Mom and Dad both called while I was at the poetry slam. Their numbers glow from my cell phone.

I know why they called. It's the first anniversary, and I should have checked in. But it will be awful to talk to them. We will have to remember what we don't want to remember. What we can't forget. It's not like we haven't been warned. The counselor also told us that it's normal to imagine the worst when we don't hear from a surviving family member. Surviving. Barely.

I flip through the list of missed calls again. David's number isn't there. He's probably thinking about the same thing I am—that day at the waterslides. Like me, he's probably replaying that moment in the day when I could have stopped her—and didn't. He was there. He knows. The knowledge binds us together even though he's in Vancouver and I'm here.

People shuffle in and out of the Koffie Klub. Sweat leaks from my pits. My bra strap has glued itself to my back. I can't go too far, but I need to move.

This month is a big one for poetry slams. Four cafés are hosting a series of competitions. They'll add up points to see who will be on the team going to Nationals. The team is organized by the Camden Slammers, a group of local poets who make the local slams happen. The slams are so popular they make almost enough at the door to pay for an all-expenses-paid trip to Corinthian for the winners. Corinthian is a small city that's being swallowed by Toronto. It may not be that far away, and putting us up might mean hostels and cheap food, but there are plenty of us who would love to go.

On good days I imagine inviting David to meet me in Corinthian. Who am I kidding? David won't be in the front row, clapping.

Anyway, I'm not good enough to make the team.

Fallout

"Don't go too far! You have another round!" Amy, one of the slam organizers yells after me. She waves when I turn to look back. "You and Ebony do the next one together, right?"

"I know!" I shout. Even if I want to walk forever, I can't let Ebony down. We've worked too hard. Returning phone calls is going to have to wait.

Poetry has taken over everything. My friendships. My spare time. My dreams. I get in trouble at the bookstore when I scribble in my notebook instead of doing my job.

Maybe I don't get paid to write poetry, but if I don't write down my ideas, they are gone. I bet half the people who work in bookstores are writers. I don't say this to my supervisor. Sometimes it's better to keep your head down and your mouth shut.

Back in the café, Ebony and I wait in the shadows at the side of the stage. Round two is about to start.

"Don't think about who's watching," Ebony says. "The judges like whatever they like."

She's right. The judges flip their plastic number cards as they listen to the poets. They hold up the scores just like in figure skating. We are here to share poetry, yes. But we are also here to win.

"Ready?" Amy says. "You guys are up next."

"Ready as I'll ever be." I like the way Ebony and I have worked this poem out. Ebony only has one word to say. She repeats it over and over. That creates a kind of rhythm, the beat for my story. We step onto the stage.

My mouth is so dry my tongue sticks to my teeth. We have up to three minutes. Three minutes can feel like forever, especially when things aren't going well. And if you go overtime? Well, the audience lets loose with a chant of:

> *You rat bastard—you're ruining it*
> *for everyone...*
> *But it was weeeelll worth it.*

I push my palms into the folds of my skirt and step up to the microphone. Ebony does the same thing a few feet away.

Ebony starts.

Ring. Ring.

Her voice is clear, beautiful. I speak next.

> *Sister, where were you when you*
> *called?*

The words take over. I move in ways I do not move unless I am in the grip of a poem.

Right on time, Ebony's voice comes in again.

Ring. Ring.
  Sister, where were you when you
    called?
  What would you have said if...

Ring.
  If I had answered the phone
  turned away from the easy heat of
    summer
  the splash of water against
  the how-much-fun-is-this slide?

Ring. Ring. Ring.
  If I had answered
  would you have told me
  your current location?
  Coffee shop?
  Street corner?
  Parking lot outside the liquor
    store
  where you smiled—actually
    smiled—

at that young man whose name
you probably never knew
though I know
and can never forget
Kenyon.

Ring. Ring.
Kenyon who had no idea
the fragile glass
the Smirnoff in the brown paper bag
would somehow survive the impact.

Kenyon. An innocent guilty young
*   man*
saw a thirsty girl
balanced on crutches
alone, a little sad. Nothing a drink
couldn't help. Nothing a favor for
*   a stranger*
or a kind word
couldn't fix.

Here, we begin to speak together.
Ebony's *Ring Ring* overlaps with my own.

> *The phone rings and rings.*
> *Ring. Ring…*

Her ringing gets louder and louder
until, at the end of the next section, we
are speaking together. Our voices are
loud and harsh and ugly.

> *If you had told me where you were*
> *would I have left behind*
> *my beach bag, sunshine, hot dog*
> *loud music, playground of*
> *The Now and come to you?*
> *Rings and rings and rings and*
> *   rings.*

> *And if I had found you,*
> *would you have told me what you*
> *   were about to do?*

Fallout

Ring. Ring.
  If you had spoken
  would I have believed you?

Ring.
  If I had believed you
  could I have stopped you?

Ring.
  Even now, three hundred and
    sixty-five
  days later
  and counting
  that phone rings

Ring.
  and rings
  day and night

Ring.
  rings through my dreams

Ring.
  rings in my morning
Ring ring ring
  ringsringsringsrings

Will it ever stop, sister?

The applause is loud when we step back from the microphones. Ebony wraps me in a tight hug.

"Good job!" she says in my ear. "Perfect."

Chapter Four

"Will you be okay, walking home alone?"

"I'll be fine." I wait with Ebony until her bus comes.

Ebony and I both did well tonight—she was third and I took fourth out of ten competing poets. The scores we got for the poem we did together don't help us against each other since we both got the same number of points. But the judges usually like good teamwork, so the higher scores are helpful against the other poets.

There were a lot of good things about tonight.

Licking whipped cream from my upper lip.

Giggling at a poem about cats and dogs running big banks.

Ebony whispering "Perfect" in my ear.

My good mood should have carried me all the way home. Instead, my phone rings somewhere deep in my purse. It's so late!

I've changed the ringtone at least twenty times in the last year but it doesn't help. If I hear the phone, something in my gut squeezes tight. No matter whose number flashes on the display, if I hear the ring I must answer.

"Hi, Mom."

"Honey—hi. How are you doing?"

She sounds like she's out of breath.

"Fine. Busy."

"How is work?" she asks.

"Fine. Busy. How about you?"

"I'm leaving for a conference in Denver tomorrow. I wanted to make sure we—talked—before I leave. I'm taking two of the senior sales guys…"

I tune out while she goes on about work. Then she switches to how she had an offer on the house that fell through. "The wife was diagnosed with breast cancer. Such a shame."

I hold the phone a little away from my ear and keep moving through the dark streets of my neighborhood. She keeps blabbing.

She has no clue she has ruined the end of my evening. Will she say something about Hannah? She almost never does. How can she go along with her oh-so-important life and never mention her other daughter? You know, the one who died? Doesn't she miss her?

"Are you still doing your poetry?"

"Hm." Mom doesn't care about poetry. She and Dad never went to my slams back when I lived at home. Mom said it gave her a headache to listen to people yelling about all the terrible things that happen in the world. "None of it rhymes!" she complained. Except for the rappers. She hated them too. They talked so fast she couldn't keep up.

After Hannah died, I knew Mom wouldn't want to hear what I had to say. I stopped inviting her and she never invited herself. Then I moved to Ontario.

She'd probably kill me if she heard the poem I performed a couple of weeks ago. Then she'd have two dead daughters she wouldn't talk about.

I can say this because you aren't here
you're in San Francisco, New York
Saskatoon, God-knows-where

Fallout

with your Yes, boss
how high, boss?
yes-men
standing at attention by your side.

"I worry about you, Tara."
I bet you do.

Does it make you feel better
taller?
smarter?
to jet off
set off
piss off
anyone who dares say
What about this way?
instead of your way?
How do you pack so much
into a carry-on bag
and a slim briefcase?
This month's sales targets
right on track.

"It seems such a waste not to be going to university."

Does it hurt to fill
your data slots
with bottom-line-driven
customer relationship management
  tools?
Forget about the mess back home.

Ignore the empty bedrooms
keep forwarding your husband's mail
ex-husband's mail
call your daughter
remind her of her duty to succeed
coach her in the ways of the world
No degree? No future.

"You can't defer your acceptance forever."
Forever is a very long time, Mom.

Move on without the life
you left behind
the day you hauled your
ass
back to the office and said
I'm fine. Let's get on with it.

Is she going to deliver the whole "such a waste" lecture? Not going to school is a waste. Me working at a bookstore is a waste. Me not living at home and spending my money on rent is a waste. How dare I waste my life when I, at least, still have one?

"Are you still there, Hannah?"

The shock of hearing her name stops me in the middle of the sidewalk.

"I mean—oh, Tara—I'm sorry. Are you still there?"

"Yes, Mom—I'm here."

"I guess I was thinking about her. I was moving those boxes in the basement into storage. One of them wasn't closed properly…"

An empty whiskey bottle stands on top of the newspaper box at the corner. It's too late and too dark to be here by myself, but my feet won't move. Now that Mom's talking about Hannah I want her to stop.

"It was a heavy box—"

"Mom, why are you telling me this?"

"Because I had to repack the stuff into two smaller boxes. One of the things I found was her riding journal. I thought you might want it—as a—as a…"

Souvenir? Could that possibly be the word she's groping for?

"Something to remind you of Hannah. Maybe I didn't do the right thing. I sent it to you."

"You what! What's in it?"

"I—I don't know. I opened one page and when I saw—when I tried to read—there were photos—I couldn't—"

At the other end of the line she sucks in a breath. Then she sighs and continues.

"What's done is done. The package is in the mail. It should arrive in a week or so. I thought I'd better warn you so you didn't get excited and think it was chocolates or something."

Chocolates? I've been living in Ontario for six months and Mom has never sent me chocolates.

"Mom—I should go. I've got to get home."

"You're still out? Are you alone?"

"I'm fine. But I should go. You're okay?"

"Yes, yes of course. Very busy. I'll call you when I get back from Denver."

We swap goodbyes and the line goes dead.

Chapter Five

In bed the next morning I lie very still.
My head pounds. A brown tabby cat
jumps into the flower box outside my
window. She looks a lot like Mishka,
a cat we once had at home.

The line between here
and nowhere
is a fine one.

Fallout

Remember Mishka?
One minute a cat crossing a lawn
following something—

How did I get from a cat at the window to a memory? And how did I get from there to a poem? The poem links one death to another. It fills the page in my notebook.

Dead in the middle of the road
thin trickle of blood
oozing out of his delicate nose.

Press his still-warm body
to my nine-year-old chest
Wait for the rise and fall of the living
wait for the stillness to burst back
    into flame
wait for the rake of claws across my
    arms
let me go let me go let me go.

Nothing moves.
Breathe, I whisper.
Breathe.

On the line
between here and nowhere
I wait for Hannah.

On my side of the line
my sister's seventeenth birthday
appears with the turn of the
    calendar page.

On her side of the line
the first anniversary
of her death.

I never saw my sister's body.
Never had a chance
to squeeze the breath
back into her.
Never had a chance
to feel the warmth easing away

*to whatever place warmth goes
when no longer needed.*

That place on her side of the line.

There are so many mysteries about
Hannah's death. The one I cannot wrap
my head around is how she pushed her
body across the line. Wasn't there a
struggle?

For the next three days I carry around
the poem about the cat and the line
between life and death. I cross things out,
move stuff, and squeeze in new lines and
extra words. Then I start to memorize
and plan how to deliver it at the next slam.

The crowd at the Xpress Yourself
Espresso Bar is silent until the last
words are done.

The applause folds around me. I'm
still wondering about Hannah's final

moments, how she found the strength to take that last step.

Clarissa, tonight's emcee, gives me a quick hug. "Good!" she whispers. Then she gently guides me off the stage.

"You're doing great," Maddy says. "How are you holding up?"

Maddy and Ebony stand on either side of me in the hallway leading to the bathroom.

"Okay," I say, though that's a lie. I am so tired I can hardly stand. Four of us are through into the last round of the evening. The points we earn tonight will keep us all in the running for the team.

I met Maddy and Ebony right after I moved here. We're in a writing group along with three other girls. The other girls don't always show up. But me, Maddy, and Ebony—we'd have to be in comas before we missed a meeting.

Ebony and I have done a few poems together, like the ringing phone we performed last week. But we're also competing against each other. Maddy doesn't have a competitive bone in her body—at least, not for herself. She's pretty loud when it comes to cheering for us.

It would be so great if both Ebony and I made the team. More likely, one of us won't survive these early rounds. It would almost be better if neither of us got to go.

I'm sure that, after the team's announced, we'll be happy for whoever gets on. For now, it's strange being supported by someone who needs to beat me. It's just as hard to smile and congratulate her after a strong round.

"Which poem are you going to do?" Maddy asks.

"The last supper poem." They've both heard all my poems in our writing group. If they disagree with my choice, they don't say.

Somehow, when I am back onstage the exhaustion fades away. From some place deep inside I find the words. They are all lined up, ready to march out into the world.

When you are hungry, eat.
  Garlic smashed potatoes
  peas and mint sauce
  roast chicken—rosemary, thyme.
  Enjoy every buttered roll
  every sprinkle of salt
  because you never know when one
    supper
  becomes the last supper.
  The last time we believe
  she might actually appear
  in time for dessert.

These are the things I wonder aloud:
  Should we wait to begin
  or start without her?
  Did she leave a message?

Fallout

Wasn't she meeting a friend?
Was she looking for a ride home?
—you know how she feels
about buses.

These are the things I wonder in
silence:
Where is she?
When will she be back?
Do I lie about hearing the phone
ring?
Is there a reason for this stab of
dread?
or is the stab of dread
something I added later
the something I should have felt.

My father out of his chair, grumbling
Telemarketers—they wait until
people are eating.
Hello? Yes—she is my daughter.
Where is she? What happened?

The serving spoon heavy in my
  hand
hangs over the bowl of mashed
  potatoes.
My mother's face, pale

    what? what is it?

my father slaps at his pockets
fumbles for his keys
    accident

    what kind of accident?

all of us running
the serving spoon still in my hand
as I reach the door
no time to go back
no time to ask questions
no time no time
I drop the spoon
sticky with the last meal
Hannah never shared with us

drop the spoon on the boot tray
scramble out the door
and into the late evening sun
fall into the rolling car
pull the door shut.

After, Maddy and Ebony wrap their arms around me. We wait to hear the results of the judging.

Chapter Six

"We have a six point seven—" Boos from the audience interrupt Clarissa when she tries to read the scores. "Applaud the poet, not the scores, people!" She wags her finger at the crowd. "A seven point five—"

"Higher!" several people yell.

"Eight point six, eight point seven, and another eight point seven."

The room explodes with cheers and hoots. Maddy's hug tightens. "You're going to make it," she says, grinning.

"Thanks," I say.

Ebony punches me lightly in the shoulder and gives me a thumbs-up. The next poet steps up to the microphone.

"Tiff is going to be hard to beat," Maddy says.

No argument there. Tiffany Hwan writes amazing poems about what it's like to be the child of immigrants.

Tiffany stands up there with a wicked twinkle in her eye. People start smiling before she even opens her mouth. She gets the room laughing within moments of starting. By the end of each poem she touches something in me even though I'm not Korean and my parents didn't come from anywhere exotic.

I'd love to be able to make people laugh, but Hannah won't let me.

Later, I check the website for the team results. Tonight I'm in third place, enough to keep me in the running.

My head aches and I dig in my purse for Tylenol. I have an early shift at the bookstore tomorrow. Rent is due next week. I can't be sick.

Are you all together?
This crisp question from a crisp nurse
at a spotless desk.
Patient privacy? Who needs privacy

when the patient is dead?

I practice in front of my bathroom mirror. A mop handle is my mic. Even though I work every day this week, I'm squeezing rehearsal time into every spare minute. I can't afford to stumble over a line at the next slam.

In the mirror I'm awkward and clumsy. I move my hands in time with the opening line of the hospital poem. A sweep of one arm shows my family gathered at the emergency room.

Hannah's family?
We nod, a family of bobbleheads.

What about Hannah?
Daughter. Sister. Child.

Where is she? What happened?

We are herded
into the quiet room
lambs to the slaughter.

Where is she?
What happened?

Nurses. Doctor. Priest.
They fill in gaps as best they can
each piece of information

She was hit in a crosswalk

balanced by more questions

Was she alone?
Was the driver drunk?
How badly hurt?

the answers an avalanche of agonies

Alone, she was alone
bus driver, devastated
your daughter
so far beyond hurt

no treatment possible
we did everything we could
a bus is no match
for a determined child.

Fallout

They throw questions back
Was she depressed?
Did she talk about hurting herself?

My mother shouting
Charge the driver!

Their reply, a question
Was there a note?

My mother asking
Did Hannah have her crutches?
as if crutches
could beat back a bus.

Someone mentions the bottle of
Smirnoff
how the thin skin of the paper bag
must have saved it.
This seems as incredible
as the idea that Hannah's skin
could not hold her together.

When can we see her?

My father's hand touching my
    mother's shoulder.
My mother's shoulder sagging
    beneath its weight.

The pastor offers solace
A doctor offers Ativan
Dad signs here
initials there
my father's legs
carry him from the room
to identify her body.
Identify. Her. Body.

Though it's much too late
my mother pleads
Please let her be okay.
Please, God, let her be okay.

Fistfuls of tissue wedged against
a river of tears so wide and so deep

we still have not reached the other side.

I step back from the mirror and sigh. It's hard to make it clear who is speaking. One more time.

Are you all together?

As my arm swings wide, the phone rings. Crap. Who could that be?

Chapter Seven

"Jesus, Tara. You gave me a fright."

Dad's words on the phone startle me. It's like he, too, is back in the hospital that day.

You gave me a fright. Those were his words when I came to after I fainted in the emergency room. The shock of hearing what happened to Hannah, I guess. When I woke up,

I was in a hospital bed. They kept me in overnight.

"I've been trying to reach you for—days."

My father's voice is worried but calm, just like the day Hannah died.

"Hi, Dad. How are you?"

When I talk to my father I have to pay attention. It's not like with Mom, who yacks on and on whether or not I'm listening. With Dad, if I don't keep things moving forward, the conversation stops.

"Dad?"

"I'm still here." There's another pause. Does he mean he's still there like a dad, available to offer words of advice and comfort? Hardly. Does he mean he's still there and hasn't blown his head off? He isn't where he is supposed to be, which is at home with his wife. Or rather, with my mother, the woman who used to be his wife.

"Playing lots of golf?" If he catches my snotty tone, he pretends not to.

"A bit."

A bit. What does that mean? That he's playing every day but doesn't want me to know? That he hasn't played since last summer, but he's still stuck back on the day his younger daughter died?

There's so much time between our comments that I could write a poem about what he might or might not be thinking. We talk so rarely there's probably a book's worth of stuff going on between phone calls.

"How's David?"

How should I answer? David and I hardly ever talk. "He's fine, I think."

"Maybe you should call him," Dad says.

Seriously? Dad's telling me to get off the phone and call my ex-boyfriend?

"Maybe."

"Okay. Good. Well, I guess that's it, then."

There's no *goodbye*, no *I love you,* no *I'm so sorry for everything I've put you through. I should never have left your mother. I should have been there for your sister. I should be there for you now.* Nothing. Just a click, a silence, and a dial tone.

I pull my notebook from my book bag and start to scribble.

My Father Is Not My Father

My father is not my father
in the way he left us
fell into the arms of
a student teacher.
How could he be so predictable
so bald—so middle-aged?

Does it matter
that his heart opening

in hotel rooms
slammed the door on my mother
my sister
on me?

My father is my father
in the way we disappear
backs turned, ears sealed.
Our desires
smother sense.

My father is my father
scotch over ice
as I am the sweet burn
of port wine.

We hold our lovers tight
in the moment before dawn
when those who miss us
ask where we've gone.

My father is not my father
but a man who once lived

Fallout

in my house—a house where
I once lived
with a dream-torn family
broken and broken again.
Whole members are missing
gone before anyone thought to say—
Hey. Don't go. Stay.

Chapter Eight

On Wednesday night Maddy and Ebony slide into a booth at Antonio's Coffee Bar and Chocolate Shoppe. Ebony and I want to check out the space before the slam on Saturday.

I slide a piece of paper across the table. "I can't get the first part right," I confess.

"Read it," Ebony says.

"Now?"

They nod, so I read, trying not to be too loud.

This Is How the World Responds

I fainted when
it sank in what Hannah had done.

When a girl
steps in front of a bus.

Some people phone
leave messages

> *I heard what happened*
> *I'm so sorry*
> *If there's anything I can do...*

Do what?
Hand us fresh tissues
when ours are so wet
they shred?

Do what?
Pat our backs, nod sadly
say, Tomorrow's tomorrow will be
    easier.

Or are you thinking of practical
    things:
dusting the family photographs
or maybe sorting through my
    sister's clothes
to see if something fits your daughter
because obviously Hannah's stuff
    won't fit me.
What a shame to waste such pretty
    things.

Some bring
food that freezes well
lots of cheese and potato
too many calories
or sweet beyond belief.

Fallout

Others hide
behind the safe walls
of distance and time.

> *I heard the news*
> *but thought it best to leave you*
> *alone.*

So many people know
our business.
So many forms to sign
payment plans to think about.
How can it cost so much
to put someone in the ground?
Don't you know that sixteen-year-olds
don't have burial plans?

What if we can't pay?
What should we do with her?
Stash her in the basement
until she gets fed up
and moves on?

In the recycling box
a headline
and a photograph:
> *An ambulance*
> *pulling away from the curb*
> *the empty bus waiting for a*
>> *new driver.*

I free the newspaper from the blue
>> *plastic box*

to save Hannah from strangers
stop her from being shredded.

She must not disappear
with all the other news of the day.

They lean back in their chairs.

"Wow," Maddy says.

Ebony nods. "That's a good one. Powerful. All these Hannah poems are powerful." She takes a swig of coffee. "No offense, but I can't decide if I wish I'd known her or I'm kind of glad I didn't."

How am I supposed to take that?
Maybe I should add a couple of lines to
the poem.

Then Ebony says, "Get rid of the
first two lines. You don't need them."

I reread the opening.

I fainted when
it sank in what Hannah had done.

"She's right," Maddy says.

The lines disappear with a strike of
my pen.

They say Hannah probably had a
drinking problem. I think of this
every time I pour myself anything
stronger than a cup of tea with honey.
Her secret drinking was only one of
so many secrets. How could we not
have known?

Out here on the balcony of my tiny apartment it's still muggy at two o'clock in the morning.

There's an empty garden chair beside me. I imagine David sitting there enjoying a beer. If I close my eyes I can almost hear his slow, steady breathing.

David sitting in the empty chair may not be likely, but it is possible. I can't say the same thing about Hannah. Why do I torture myself by imagining her beside me? I do it all the time. Sometimes Hannah laughs and goofs around and tells terrible jokes the way she used to. Sometimes she tells me about school, her return to riding, some new boyfriend. The details are different every time. It gets harder and harder to picture what might have been. Would she have gone to university to study sports medicine like she'd always planned? Might she have fallen in love and had a baby? Or bought a Great Dane? She always wanted a dog.

"You want to hear a poem, Hannah?" I ask the empty chair. I raise my glass in her direction. "No, this time it isn't about you. I wrote it a while back, before I left the coast. Yes, it's about David. Too bad you guys never got along."

I speak softly, as if I really am confiding in my sister.

Leave him, cut him loose
send him
into his bright future.

Look at me. Twenty-five pounds more
miserable, sucking back the booze
lusting after double chocolate-chip
*   cookies*
Extra Crisp potato chips
whipped cream waffles and bacon
*   sandwiches.*

Look at him, looking at me, thinking
he's stuck with twenty-five bonus
    pounds
of difficult to swallow.

Leave, and we can finish falling
land where we will land
broken or bent.
I'm tired of trying to fit two huge
    truths
that I killed her
and that he knows I killed her
into one relationship too small to
    hold all that sadness.

And another truth,
He was there too
not answering his phone.
He laughed
when I laughed and said
Not today, Hannah. Today you
    won't take us

*away from each other, tear us from
our place in the sun.*

The darkness presses close. Splats of
warm rain smack my bare arms.

"What do you say to that, Hannah?
Is that what you had in mind when you
walked away? Did you hate him that
much? Did you hate me that much?"

I flinch when a bolt of lightning
crackles across the sky.

Dripping wet, I retreat into the
apartment and sink onto the mattress.
For a long time I listen to the rain
punish the world.

Chapter Nine

Everything is poetry. If I am not onstage,
I am practicing. I yell the words into the
wind down at the lake. I whisper them
into my pillow before I fall asleep.

> *Normal is taking a long shower*
> *loud music cranked so high*
> *it's louder than the water splashing*
> *but all you hear later is*

Fallout

How about leaving some hot water
*   for the rest of us?*

When you can't be normal anymore
your father pounds on the locked
*   door*
calling your name
calling your name
calling your name
panic stenciled over his heart
not again not again
Answer me or I'm breaking down
*   this door!*

Stepping naked from the shower
skin reddened from the hot water
I reach for the towel on the back of
*   the shaking door and*
yell back, Can't I have a shower in
*   peace?*
Step back into the steam.
The burning rage of the water
slices over my tender skin.

I want to pull the words
back.
Can't.

The poems carry me through the aisles at the bookstore. They keep me company on the bus.

I have measured my year in firsts
the first time I came home—after
     Hannah died
the scent of hospital in my hair·
the first bagel pushed into the toaster
inedible
tossed into the garbage despite a
     hollow ache
that grew and grew and grew
and grows even now

I capture thoughts, single words and endless lines in small notebooks. I even write on the inside of my wrist.

Fallout

the first time I showered
and wondered whether to leave
   enough hot water
for her

the first time we didn't buy school
   supplies
because she wasn't here and I
   wasn't going back
the first Halloween without costumes
shutting off the porch light
closing the drapes
and hiding upstairs
my mother and I hushing each other
as if somehow the ghosts could get
   inside
and discover our stupid lie.

I shout, weep, bleed the year in poems.

The first Christmas
her birthday

the events getting bigger
before I notice that
Hannah is missing things
she shouldn't be missing.

The first time it happened
was last summer when
I stopped, mid-sentence
and almost said aloud
Saturday won't work—
because Hannah won't be here

won't be here to attend the funeral.
Back when Hannah was so close to
*   being here*
it seemed impossible she
was really gone.

There's a huge crowd at Antonio's when the first poet begins. It's Sam, an old biker with so many tattoos it looks like he's wearing a long-sleeved shirt under his leather vest. He's a regular and does a lot of love poems that rhyme.

When it's my turn I do the poem about how the world reacts to a suicide. I've chopped the first lines and added three others.

New friends are torn between
wanting and not wanting
to have known her.

What will Ebony think? When I join her at the table she smiles.

In the second round I let fly with "She Comes Bearing Gifts."

My sister had friends
once
lots of them
before she stopped
having friends, that is
long before she stopped
being.

Jackie Lisa Tiffany Brandon
Jordan, Max and Xan
faded away
when she stopped taking their calls
never had them in
never went out.

Until that day
when she met friends for coffee.
How could such an ordinary thing
be so heavy with the thousand hints
    we missed?

What we wanted to see was
what she wanted us to see.
She was getting better
she'd turned that corner into the light
right into the coffee shop where
oh, yes, her friends are waiting
because that's what normal girls do
chat over lattes
hold the foam add the whip
skim mocha soy extra hot.

Fallout

Sometimes they give each other
    gifts, don't they?

Only for that extraspecial
tell ya anything, hon
never let you go, BFF.

For her, the world
the silver horseshoe earrings from
    Nana.
A small gift the least you can do
a thank-you
for being there when it mattered.

Jackie told me they were glad to
    hear from Hannah
she seemed more like the old Hannah
the can-I-have-a-bite-of-that?
    Hannah
the you'll-never-believe-what-
    he-said Hannah
the Hannah we knew was in there
    somewhere, right?

Jackie insisted she should have
   known
was closest
knew Hannah best—
Didn't we all think we knew her
   best—
should have known that earrings
   were more than earrings
that small gifts in the hands of
   someone on the exit ramp
are not small at all?

On the night the relatives start to
   arrive
Jackie hands me the earrings.
Nestled in their blue velvet box
like tiny sleeping memories
they curl tight into silver slivers
so sharp they bite through my mask
   send
hairline cracks pulsing through
my carefully made-up calm.

Chapter Ten

Round three is brutal. I'm up last and have to listen to everyone else. When it's my turn I clutch the mic and bring it close to my mouth. Too close. There's a squeal of feedback.

"Owww!"

"Turn it down!"

Not a good start. I hope the crowd remembers enough of the poem from

the last round that this one will make
sense. It's risky to continue a story from
one poem to another. Each should stand
alone—but these are part of a series and
I don't dare change the plan now.

The relatives arrive
trailed by small bags.
Bump up the stairs
trundle down the hall
into the den
the family room
my room
any room
but her room.

They come in clumps
mother father brother
cousin uncle aunt grandmother
fold their arms around me
because now, after her death
suddenly it's okay to touch the one who
doesn't like to hug.

Fallout

They ask, without asking
What the hell happened here?
Is it true what I read about the
    bottle of booze?
Is it true she didn't look back when
    she stepped
out
into the road?

They came because
that's what happens
when someone dies.
They gather to tell stories
slide trays of food into the fridge
because food poisoning at a time
    like this
would be unfortunate.
Who would attend the funeral?

Unspoken questions like
Should there be a funeral?
lurk in the corners
inhabited by God.

Nana's God
who apparently doesn't admit
that some of his fallen angels
jumped.

What about the casket? she asks.
Open or closed?
The guest list? How public
do we want to make this thing?

This thing?
Hello?

But how can I say anything
when she sees the blue velvet box
on the kitchen counter
folds her polished fingernails
over its curved lid and
hands shaking
stares as if it might
reveal secrets
only she can understand.

Tears wobble, glassy and fragile
on her lower lids.
I reach out.
Touch her hand.

The next morning I jolt awake. Someone is pounding on my apartment door.

"Don't let it get to you," Ebony says when I let her in.

"Easy for you to say." Last night the judges didn't like the "Relatives" poem and I didn't make it into the fourth round.

She grins and holds out a travel mug full of coffee. "This should perk you up."

"Smells good," I mumble. Ebony did well last night. She's third overall in the standings. I'm hovering in and out of fourth place. After last night, I'm out, though not by much.

"If you have a good week, you'll make it," she says.

"Maybe."

"You don't work today, do you?" Ebony asks.

"No."

"We should do something fun."

A strand of hair falls into my eyes and I push it away. How can I be so tired?

"Fun? Like what?"

"I don't know. Hunt for treasure at the thrift store?"

I sigh. "I should try to write."

"You should try *not* to write," she counters. "Even *I* don't write all the time. I know, what about—"

The phone rings.

"Sorry—I should—"

"Do you want me to go?" she asks.

"It's okay," I say and pick up the phone.

"Hey, Tara—"

"David!"

Ebony's eyebrows shoot up.

"Hey—it's been a while."

"Yeah."

"Yeah."

God. How awkward can a conversation be? "Where are you?"

"Vancouver, of course. Where else?"

Where else. "So, what's up?" I ask.

"Not much. You?"

"Work. Slams. Are you still playing soccer?" I know he is. I follow the team online. He's still one of the best in the league.

"Yeah. I had three scholarship offers for this year."

"Nice. Are you accepting any of them?"

"South Carolina. Full ride."

"Wow. Congratulations!" I hope I sound more excited than I feel. South Carolina. That's a long way from everywhere.

"So, anyway, I mostly wanted to call and say hi—you know, see if you're doing okay."

My throat closes and I can't speak. I turn away from Ebony.

"Tara? You're doing okay, aren't you?"

I hear the terror in his voice. It's what we all feel when someone doesn't pick up the phone or when a silence goes on for too long. I clear my throat. "Sorry. I'm—I'm fighting off a cold. I'm fine."

"Good. That's good."

"You?"

"I'm doing okay."

"Good." Did we really miss curfews because we couldn't stop talking? "David, I have to go. My friend's here and—"

"No problem. I just wanted to say hi." He sounds relieved.

"Thanks for calling. Talk to you soon."

We both hang up. We won't talk again for a long time.

"Aw, honey—come here," Ebony says, her arms wide. I fall against her, sobbing. She pats my back.

"Oh god—I'm sorry," I say, gulping back tears.

"No apology needed. Go wash your face. Let's go to the farmer's market."

Grateful not to be in charge, I head into the bathroom to pull myself together.

Chapter Eleven

"Have you ever had Maya's samosas?"

We're in front of a food cart in the middle of the market. "I don't think so."

"Oh my god—so good!" Ebony buys a plateful of vegetarian samosas.

We sit side by side on a bench. She holds the paper plate between us. "Careful," she says, biting off two corners of a samosa. She blows gently into one hole, forcing steam out the second. "Hot!" she says, bugging her eyes out.

"These *are* good," I agree. I love samosas, but Maya's are amazing. Potatoes, onions, peas, cilantro, a bit of curry, something peppery…"Oh, yum!"

Ebony carefully nibbles her way into the hot filling. "So, you going to tell me about this David boy?"

"Not so much to tell, really."

"How did you meet?"

I blush. "It's kind of a lame story."

"No such thing as a lame story when it comes to looove."

"You haven't heard it yet…"

"So tell me."

"Everybody at my school knew David. He's a really good soccer player and he's also smart and funny—and, you know, self-confident."

Ebony grins. "Sounds like Mr. Perfect."

"Almost."

"Have another one before I eat them all. So he went to your school and you and every other girl thought he was amazing. How did you—?"

"We were at this dance. A group of us girls—we were all dancing together. Then about four of the soccer players joined us—and somehow David and I started dancing."

Ebony waits for me to go on.

"This is going to sound so bad—"

"I doubt it. We've all been there."

"It was hot, so after three dances we went outside to cool off. He said he liked the way I moved—"

"Oooh…"

"And he asked me if I needed a drink—"

"I bet you did—"

"Well, yeah. So we went back to his car and I gulped this beer down way too fast and then…"

Ebony giggles. "Okay, I get it."

"I don't. Not really. I always thought I was the kind of girl who wanted to have a conversation first—Shut up! It's not that funny!"

"Sorry. So you guys did it in the parking lot?"

My head feels like it's going to fall off. What am I doing telling her all this? "Well, more or less."

"And?"

"What, and?"

"You must have liked more-or-lessing with him—you kept seeing him, right?"

"Yeah. We were together two years."

"That's a lot of more-or-lessing!"

She's right. We spent a *lot* of time more-or-lessing.

"Did you like it?"

Oh god. Why did I let her start down this path? Yes, I liked it. A lot. It was the best part of our relationship.

It wasn't like he was into poetry, and I don't think I ever watched a whole soccer game. How sad is that?

Ebony ignores my failure to answer and keeps right on going.

"Because there's nothing wrong with enjoying yourself. Why should guys have all the fun?" She chomps down on another samosa. "Oh. My. God. These are *so* good. We should try to make them sometime."

"Really? Do you really think that?" I ask.

"What—that we should make samosas? Or that girls can like sex as much as boys? I'm not going to speak for everyone, but sure—I mean, as long as you're careful and everybody plays nice and you both want to…"

I can't believe we're having this conversation sitting on a Camden park bench. Mom would be horrified.

"Not everybody agrees," I say.

"Who cares? You're not trying to make other people happy. That's the fast road to hell, if you ask me."

"Split the last one?"

We tear the last samosa down the middle and sit side by side, chewing.

"It's not fair what some people say about girls like us," Ebony says, wiping her fingers on her jeans.

I know exactly what she means. "There's a difference between lusty and wicked—"

"Stop! You should write that down!"

"I've wanted to do a poem about this forever," I confess.

"Say it again."

"There's a difference between lusty and wicked…"

"How about this—*Who says that lusty implies some kind of wicked?* Is it better when you start with a question?"

"What do you think?"

"Maybe. Then you could go on with something like, *are lusty women lewd or*—"

"Lascivious," I suggest.

"Lascivious?"

"Too hot for your own good."

"Hang on. Let's write this down."

I pull my notebook from my bag and open it on my lap.

We work together for almost an hour, throwing ideas back and forth. Ebony takes the page and writes; I take it back and write. When we're done we have a long poem in two voices about— well, all kinds of things.

"We could perform this at Nationals," Ebony says. "If we both make the team. God, I really hope we both do."

"Me too."

"Let's do it one more time," she suggests. "Then I have to go."

I have no idea who hears our poem, and I don't care. We read through it together as if we've been practicing for years. Sometimes she reads alone, sometimes I do. Then, somehow, we both know when we need to deliver a line together.

Who says that lusty implies
some kind of wicked?
that women are lewd
or lascivious
when, in fact, exuberant
is not lawless
extravagant
not the same as careless.

Immoral, or frolicsome?
Unchaste, or playful?
We choose playful and yet
we see how they look at us when

> *when my hand slides under his*
> *shirt*
> *rests gently against the warm*
> *skin of his back.*

when I slip my hand in his
in the lobby of the Grand Plaza
    Hotel.

Your lover is a boy
mine is a man
gentle and sophisticated.
He knows his wines
cars
cruise lines
and corporate logos.

My boy knows my body.
Whatever electric pulses
hormones
or destiny
were at work on the dance floor
at the high school gym
left us sweating in the backseat
    of his car.

Three years ago
it seemed that fate

Fallout

had delivered my boy
into my lap
his curly hair tickling my chin
as he nuzzled his way
into cleavage
and I sighed my way into
    oblivion.

My gentleman friend
understands the language of
    chocolates
roses shipped by the dozen.

My boy understands the
    language of soccer
shoots to score
leaves his cleats
on the floor by the bed
and whoops when he should
    whisper.

There's no way to speak of this
without moaning

the pleasure of memory
the way the windows fogged
the way the springs heaved us
    back and forth
the way he had to move the
    umbrella
before someone got hurt.

Lace and small buttons
    soccer cleats and hockey jerseys
snaps and scarves
    jeans so tight you can't help
        but squeeze

    Always a drink before
Always a drink after

The hostess greets him by name
Good evening, Mr. Charmante...
wine list
specials.
I am special

Fallout

his lovely girl
elegant in pearls
and pumps
and a simple black dress
he will peel off
as I loosen his tie.

It was all so easy, remember?

Of course you remember
the line in the sand
the very minute when

it stopped being easy

the evening I
picked up the cell phone
and heard his wife's voice

the day we didn't answer our
*   phones*
and kept on playing.

You remember when we started being
something else:
an obligation
born not of pleasure
but of shared guilt
knowing that the world

divides

into two kinds of people
those who know
    those who have wives
    and those who don't

those who have killed
and those who haven't
    those who tell the truth
    and those who make love with
        lies
those who know what it is to be left

    and those who believe
    that leaving is easy.

Chapter Twelve

Later, when I'm back at home, I wonder if it does any good to spew this stuff all over our audience. Who cares about that first time in David's car? And what about Ebony's married gentleman friend? How does it help anyone to know any of this?

These questions scribble their way into my journal. I'm left with the thought that I will never know who is listening. Maybe some girl who is churning inside with guilt because she enjoys her boyfriend's tongue just a little too much might realize she's not alone. Maybe some girl who's thinking things will be better after she takes those pills will hesitate long enough to get some help.

"Ta-ra! Ta-ra! Ta-ra!"

Ebony and Maddy start the chant. Others in the packed coffee shop join in.

The scalding water
can't mask this other pain
can't stop the bus
rolling into the shower stall.

Number 7
Courtland-Downtown
the driver's face
a moon in the window.

Fallout

one two three
Maybe she counted
then gave herself a shove.
Maybe she fell
her poor balance, the crowds…

An old man swears he heard her cry
   out
a teenager claims silence.

Whatever she said or didn't say
whatever she thought or didn't think
whatever hesitation, good sense
   regret
second thoughts
drowned out
by the squeal of bus brakes.

   watch out!
   stop!

bus driver leaping out of his seat
tie flying behind him

someone holding one of Hannah's
  crutches
though it is obvious crutches won't
  be much use
to the crumpled, bleeding body so
  still on the road

Cell phones snap open
Nine-one-one emergency. Do you
  need police, fire or ambulance?
The crowd pushing in

  What happened?
    A girl just got hit by a bus
  Did she fall?
  Will she be okay?

Of course not—
the angle of the neck
the shattered skull.
Everything. Everything about this
  girl is broken.

Fallout

In the shower
the heat
the steam
the water
the endless hot tears
swirl through and around and into
   me
into the street scene so real
that sometimes I wonder
Should I stay unclean?

Snap the taps back off
wrap the towel around me
sink to the floor
a locked door between me and
all those funeral preparations
relatives hunched over the dining
   room table
struggling to write the obituary
waiting for me to join them
to help honor the life that was my
   sister's.

She checked out
made it easy on herself.

But what about us?
What about me?
The way forward, through the
    bathroom door
littered with saying the wrong thing
smiling when the last thing I want
    to do is smile.
The way back, through time, a
    minefield of
what-ifs
if-onlys
I-should-haves.

Or I can stay here
in the quiet of this small room
until someone panics
breaks down the door.

The applause carries me back to our table.

"Good job," Maddy says. "You'll get through to round two for sure."

Ebony nods. "Shh. Karl's up."

Karl explodes with a poem about two Germanys before the Berlin Wall was taken down.

Shoot. Shoot. Shoot to kill.
We protect our citizens
keep them safe behind the wall.

Ebony is next. Her whole body lifts into the poem. Her mother black, her father white, she lives in a simmering space between. The words tumble and roll around her. She rises up onto her toes, her hips moving this way and that. She is fierce in the challenges she throws at us.

People shout and bang mugs on tables even before the last words fade away. She drops her face into her hands and backs away from the mic. When she slides back into the empty seat beside me, she cannot suppress a smile.

"Good," I say. "You made it."

She crosses her fingers and holds them high.

Six of us move on to the second round of the night. Everyone is sharp and hungry.

Blake, tonight's emcee, says, "Please welcome Tara Manson."

This is what's in the mail:
Two men and a strong ladder
to fix your gutter
hungry students to paint your house.
Phone bill. VISA statement.
Who cares? stuff
arrives every day.

Then, a fat envelope
soft with crinkles as if
it had been well-handled
or stuffed in a backpack

or hidden under a mattress
or all of the above.

Addressed to me.

It isn't my name
that hits me like a punch to the gut.
It's the loopy handwriting
a heart over the letter i
each time it appears.

Wild thoughts crash into each other
a hailstorm
of jumbled questions.

Where is Hannah writing from?
If the girl in front of the bus wasn't
    Hannah
then who?

On my bed
legs crossed
hands quivering

I tear open the envelope and
tug out the contents
start with the letter
written—in haste?
With plenty of time to consider?

> *Dear Tara*
> *By the time you read this*
> *I will be gone.*
> *Don't be sad it's better like this.*
> *It doesn't matter if I am*
>   *around anymore*
> *you and Mom and Dad*
>   *deserve to be happy*
> *it's bad that you are always*
>   *worrying about me.*

She goes on to explain
no friends no life no hope no future
nothing but some kind of dark hole
where she has no interest in staying.
She doesn't expect me to understand.

Fallout

I am a drain on you and
* everyone.*
I know you are trying to help
but that isn't your job.
You will be happy at university
and this way you don't need to
* worry.*
If I do this now
you won't have to miss
any school for the funeral.

As if missing school for the funeral
might have been a hardship
as if going to a funeral
is something you want to do
instead of other things
as if there's no contest
as if this is a logical choice
Stupid stupid stupid ass.

I love you forever and always
your sister
Hannah

I turn it over and over and over
looking for more—over and over—
trying to find Hannah
over and over—
Written on the back
of a fast-food restaurant tray liner
the note dodges grease spots.

The page swims before my eyes
wobbly, uncertain
real and final.

Tucked into the envelope
a napkin
scarred with chicken-scratch lists

> *Dad*
> *Cash (not much, sorry*
>   *look in my purse, bank*
>   *account closed)*
> *School books and papers*
>   *(or just burn them)*

I hear the or whatever *she has
not added.*

> *Mom*
> *Books*
> *Riding ribbons, trophies*
>   *etcetera*

> *Tara*
> *Riding stuff (I think it's all
>   down in the basement)*
> *Earrings (except for horse-
>   shoes—those to Jackie)*
> *Books (share with Mom)*
> *Clothes (or give away to
>   charity)*

*The pen had skipped and blotted
over her last will and testament
scribbled in a booth?
on a hard plastic seat?
at the bus stop?*

107

Earrings. Books. Clothes.
Did she expect us to appreciate
this thoughtful gesture?
Did she imagine we'd be thankful that
even in her time of despair
she was thinking of us
when, clearly, she was not thinking
* of us at all*
or she would have known that this
* pitiful offering*
was so shallow—so selfish
a transparent attempt to ease her
* conscience*
by tidying up her room
putting her affairs in some kind of
* order.*

My name is on the envelope
and this is how it slips under my
* lacy bras*
and silk panties
tucks into a dark corner and rests
* there awhile*

until the time comes
to share this last moment of
    Hannah's
with the handful of others
who need to know.

Chapter Thirteen

Slams are different from regular poetry readings. At an old-fashioned poetry reading the audience is polite even when the poetry sucks. At a slam, crowds sometimes hiss and boo. Things aren't quite that bad tonight, but I'm not surprised when my name is not one of the four second-round winners.

Ebony advances and so does a skinny guy called Mike. He looks about twelve but he's actually twenty. Mike is hilarious. He does a poem about the war between a procrastinator and his conscience. We're all grabbing for napkins so we don't spray our drinks everywhere.

Karl, the German guy, moves on, even though I don't think his second poem is that great. Rosie, the fast-talking food girl, is the fourth poet to survive to round three.

It's a relief, in a way, to be able to sit back and listen.

The last round is intense. Ebony does a great job with a poem about the pleasures of sleep. I doubt I'm the only one ready for bed by the time she's done. Even though Karl's poem about a puppet is really clever, he doesn't stand a chance, and Ebony winds up being the big winner of the night.

"Congratulations," I say. "Nice," I add, examining her gift basket. It's full of fancy chocolates and good coffee. She also won the big cash prize of thirty-five bucks.

"Thanks," she says, smiling. "Sorry about tonight."

I shrug. "It's okay," I say, though it isn't.

The organizers of the slam series are over behind the counter, punching calculator buttons. Tonight's the night they announce the team. It would be better to know if I'm not going. We all hold hands under the table when the emcee, Blake, steps up on the stage and grabs the mic.

"What an exciting series this has been. Let's have a round of applause for all the poets."

I squeeze Ebony's hand and she squeezes back.

"As I announce the winners' names, please come up here onstage so we can share the love!" Hoots and whoops fill the coffee shop. "The following fine poets will represent our fair city at the National Poetry Slam to be held in Corinthian two weeks from now!"

"Karl Meisner—"

"I knew he'd make it," Maddy says.

"Tiffany Hwan. And...Ebony Graham."

I let go of Ebony's hand. "Congratulations!"

Ebony's huge grin says it all.

"We have an odd situation here," Blake says as Ebony joins the others onstage. "We have a tie for fourth place—Tara Manson and Rosie McCarthy. Would you lovely ladies please join us up on stage?"

Stunned, I do as I'm told.

"We're allowed to send four team members and one alternate. One of you two will be our fourth and the other the alternate, and..." Blake shuffles through his papers and then asks Geoff, who's in charge of the sound system, "What did we decide?"

"We didn't!" Geoff booms from the back of the room. "We'll figure out a fair way to choose our fourth, but either way, you're both going to Nationals."

That seems to be enough to satisfy the crowd, and the place erupts into a wild frenzy of cheers and clapping.

Ebony gives me a huge hug. "Two weeks!" she says. "Corinthian, here we come!"

Back at our table, we're joined by the other team members and a skinny boy I've seen before but have never met.

"They should have just picked one of us," Rosie says. She probably means they should have picked her. "It's not fair to not know who's on and who's not."

"You're both going," Ebony says. "They have special events for the alternates."

"So cool you get to go again," the skinny boy says. Karl is the only one who has been to Nationals before.

"Do you guys all know my brother, Ossie?" he asks, nudging the skinny boy with his elbow.

We exchange greetings and order another round of drinks. It's late and we're still buzzing when the baristas start sweeping up around us.

"Do you want to walk home?" Ebony asks.

"Good plan." I'm wide awake now.

"I can walk with you as far as the train station," Rosie says.

I don't know Rosie very well. Chatting with Ebony won't be the same. Then again, we're sort of teammates, so I suck it up and say, "Sure. You live over that way?"

"On Fifth. About two minutes from the station."

Everyone else fades into the night and we head down Bingham Street. A light rain starts to fall when we take the shortcut through the park.

"What poem were you going to do if you'd made it through to the last round tonight?" Ebony asks.

Is she wondering if I performed the right pieces? If I had done things a little differently, maybe I would have had the extra point I needed to make the team. We're supposed to find out about the final decision at a team meeting in two days. How are they going to decide?

"I was going to do 'Obituary.'"

"Is that the one where your family is fighting about what to put in the paper?"

"That's the one."

"Can you do poetry and walk at the same time?" Ebony asks.

"That's okay. I'm sure Rosie doesn't want to—"

"No, go ahead." Rosie's slow to say it.

Ebony barges in. "Don't be shy! Go on. There's nothing like an obituary poem to take your mind off the rain!"

Rosie shoves her hands deep in her pockets and keeps walking.

"You might need to do it at Nationals. Every chance to practice is good, right?"

I can't argue with that. "Fine."

The dark shapes of trees and bushes are hiding places for who knows what kinds of people that haunt the park at night. The louder I am, the more likely I'll scare them off.

Fill in the blanks
and come up with an acceptable
    obituary.
Our beloved so-and-so
taken too early
to return to God
leaving behind

loving husband wife
two sons a daughter
grandchildren
a dog

...after a valiant battle
cancer, stroke

Lived a full and happy life
old age.

Thank you to the caring staff
the loving helpers at hospice
instead of flowers
donations to this charity
in the name of Uncle Jack
we have established a fund.

A celebration of life will be held
on the mountaintop she loved best
at such-and-such a church, funeral
*   home*

Fallout

pay your respects, share your
    memories
we'll scatter the ashes at sea.

What obituaries do not say is
Uncle Edward died by his own hand
unable to see his way clear of debt.
Following a struggle with depression
the demons finally got to Father
the bastards sucked him into the
    barrel of a gun.

There is no mention of the broken
    brains
drowning in voids so black
the only way out lies at the end of a
    noose
or in the path of an oncoming bus.

Where are those deaths?
Where is the S-word
in this public listing of grief?

This collection of acceptable ends
shameful the way it
leaves out those
who just could not go on
twice erased
but never forgotten.

The reason lies in the mothers
sisters fathers holy men who say
there are right ways to die
and then there are sins.

This is true even for non-believers
like my mother
who sweeps the scribbled draft
off the dining room table and
*   declares*
the bus driver a murderer
at least guilty of manslaughter—
*   A leave of absence in no way*
*   compensates for what he has*
*   done to this family.*

Fallout

Her logic sound because
There was no note.

Except, there is a note
slim and invisible in my underwear
*   drawer.*

What made me
march upstairs
to retrieve that package
slide it across the table
and watch it come to rest in front of
*   her?*

What sense of justice
*   grow up*
*   get on with it*
*   act like the adult*
*   you are supposed to be*
made me spit out the words
*   There's your note.*

By the time you read this
I will be gone.
Don't be sad it's better like
    this.

The reading of it
Dropped my mother
carried her out of the room
on a wave of wailing
sobs shaking her body
    Someone killed my baby.
    Someone should pay.

You won't find any of that
splashed across
the back pages of the paper
no matter how closely you read
between the lines
looking for stories of those
who met an unexpected end.

I finish as we stop at the corner at the north end of the park. Ebony is quiet,

shipping boots from dryer
extra water bucket

The list is a full page long, and beside each item she added a tiny smiley face instead of a tick mark.

I stop reading. The next day, everything changed. If I don't turn the page, I can fill my head with the Hannah who still made lists, had plans and thought Crackerjack was the best horse ever.

Chapter Fifteen

There is no holding back time—
not then, not now. I turn the page, not
really wanting to know what Hannah
had written next, but curious. I thought
maybe she would have written about
the surgery, her time in intensive care,
her move to the rehab hospital. Maybe
she did write about that somewhere,

but not in this journal. Here, the next entry is dated a little more than three months after the accident. It's all about the day Mom and I took Hannah to the barn for a visit. It had been my idea.

Saw Crackerjack today. Some lady is riding him.

Hannah was still in a wheelchair. We didn't know if she'd ever walk again. The physiotherapists pushed her hard and Hannah seemed to be up to the challenge. I remember once she said, "Even if I could walk with crutches, I'd be happy."

She didn't write again until about a year after the accident.

Things I Can't Do

1. Stand. Must hang on to something or I topple over. Need crutches and leg braces.

2. Walk. Obvious, if I can't stand. What I do is way beyond a limp.

She goes on and on, a dark list of loss. My throat tightens. Why did Crackerjack have to fall? Why didn't Hannah sail off, as she had plenty of times before, and suffer nothing more serious than a few cuts and bruises?

I flip to the next page, and it's like Hannah throws acid in my face.

Read this, Tara. You proved that I am finished as a rider. You helped me see there really is no point going on. For that, I thank you.

Oh god. The blood drains from my head so fast the room tilts.

You helped me see there really is no point going on.

She must have been talking about the few lessons I'd arranged with her old coach, Rena. Rena and I had worked out what horse Hannah would ride, how to get her mounted, how to help her come back to the world she loved.

But in the end, everything I had tried to do was so, so wrong.

You helped me see...

How could I have been so stupid?

For the next couple of days I march from place to place like a zombie. At the bookstore I ask the customers, "Bookmark? Did you find everything you were looking for? Bag? Cash, credit or debit?"

I ask myself, Did Mom read what Hannah wrote? Did Hannah mean for me to read her journal? If she didn't, why did she write it? And if it's true what she wrote, and if, say, the police read it, does it somehow make me responsible? If I caused her suicide, then am I a murderer?

At home I cook—lentil soup, three-bean chili, stuffed baked potatoes.

I clean the bathroom, sweep off the balcony, dig out my sweaters from the storage locker in the basement. I crank up my MP3 player and try to drown out any words with a roar of music. Hard as I try to shut them out, Hannah's words push through.

You helped me see there really is no point going on.

What did she want me to do with those words? Apologize? How? She bailed on whatever conversation we might have had.

Screw you, Hannah! I take shower after shower, each one hotter than the one before. What do you want me to do, Hannah? Follow you? I don't know if I can.

Is this how she felt? Desperate? Her guts churning?

I polish the bathroom mirror and stack the spare toilet paper rolls in a neat pyramid. If I follow Hannah,

I will not leave a mess behind. I tidy and organize and talk to Hannah, asking her questions she refuses to answer.

I don't answer my phone or check my email. I don't do poetry.

On Friday, the night of the team meeting, I pretend to be sick. Rosie can go. I don't care.

I'm in bed when someone bangs on the door. Ebony's voice is loud out in the hallway. "Open up!" *Bang. Bang. Bang.*

They're all there. The whole team plus Ossie and Maddy. Ebony barges in.

"Welcome to Tara's place," she says. "Maybe you should get dressed?"

Bare feet, pajama bottoms, baggy T-shirt. Crap! I retreat into my bedroom, smoothing down my hair. Stupid Ebony. What the—?

"Hurry up in there," she calls. "We're hungry! We want to order something in."

I think of all the food I've been cooking. "Don't! I'll be right out."

Fifteen minutes later we're all crowded around my dining room table.

"This is really good," Karl says, polishing off his second piece of apple pie.

Ebony nods and adds, "We decided to bring the team meeting to you."

"You know it's almost midnight, right?"

"We won't get rowdy," Ossie says, grinning.

"They've decided you and Rosie are going to compete at Persephone's on Sunday," Ebony says. "The winner will take the last spot."

"Sunday? As in the day after tomorrow?"

"That's usually how it goes," Karl says.

"Are you okay with that?" I ask Rosie.

She shrugs. "It's not like we have any choice."

"I haven't been to Persephone's for a long time," I confess. I clear my throat. "Maybe Rosie should just take the last spot."

Rosie picks at the edge of a placemat.

"For the good of the team—I'll never be able to—" I stumble over my words. Make the poems harsh enough. Beautiful enough. Clever, funny, deep, whatever enough.

"No more talk of that!" Ebony says. "You're both going to Nationals—you both need to be ready. Persephone's is extra practice."

Rosie nods.

"So it's settled. We'll all be there on Sunday. Don't let us down," Ebony says.

"Fine. Okay." What Ebony and the others don't know is that's what I do best: let people down.

Thump. Thump.

"What's that?" Ossie asks, looking around.

"Upstairs neighbors," I say, pointing at the ceiling. "You guys should go."

"But we just got here!" Ebony says. She's too loud, apparently. The upstairs neighbors pound on the floor again.

"That's harsh," Ossie says.

"It's an old building," I say. "Not much insulation."

"Sorry. We never planned to eat and run," Karl says.

Before I know it the dishes are stacked and everyone's at the door saying goodbye.

Chapter Sixteen

On Sunday, Rosie jogs into the bus shelter.

"Oh. Hi."

It figures we'd be taking the same bus up to the university district. They don't run that often on Sundays.

We sit side by side on the hard wooden bench. Maybe she'll chat about the weather or how the bus is running late. No such luck.

"I'm sorry I ran out of the coffee shop the other night."

"That's okay. I get it."

"It's just…well, your poems bring up a lot of stuff for me."

"I'm sorry."

"I don't want an apology. I want to explain—"

I'm not sure I want to hear whatever she has to say.

"My aunt—the one who…died—she wasn't like a regular aunt. I mean, she was, but she was more like a second mom to me and my brothers. She was my mom's sister and she lived with us. Because my mom worked full-time to support us, Auntie Erica was always there. She helped raise us, you know?"

"Your dad didn't live with you?"

She shakes her head. "We joked about how Auntie Erica liked her quiet time in the evenings. We weren't supposed to bother her when her door was shut."

A chill passes through me. How many times did I stand outside Hannah's door, wanting to knock but not wanting to upset her? Even worse, how many times did I walk past, relieved I didn't have to deal with her sour moods?

"Then one morning a week before Christmas she didn't come downstairs. My mom had already left for work. Auntie Erica was supposed to drive us to school. It was still dark, and when I went in her room I thought she was sleeping. She wasn't sleeping."

Rosie's voice has dropped so low I have to lean close to hear her. I put my arm around her shoulder. She shrugs my hand away.

"Booze and pills. She had puked all over her bed. My mom still says it was an accident, that Auntie Erica had always had trouble sleeping."

"Look who's here!" I say, interrupting.

Rosie looks lost for a moment, and then relieved. "Hey, Ossie. You going to Persephone's? Where's Karl?"

"He got called in to work." Ossie shoves his hands deep into his pockets. "I'm here to, you know, support you guys."

We step out of the shelter and onto the sidewalk when the bus comes around the corner. The massive front end bears down on us. I draw in a sharp breath and stop, heart pounding. It's okay. The bus won't drive over the curb and crush me. I'm not going to fall into the road. I am not like Hannah. What if I lose my balance? What if someone pushes me? If the worst happens, everyone will think I did the same thing as Hannah. They'll look for a note, they'll search for reasons, they'll—

A gentle pressure on my elbow breaks through the panic. "Where's your bus pass?" Ossie asks.

Right. That's what normal people think about when a bus stops. My heart slows a little and I reach for the handrail with one hand, root around in my bag with the other.

Ossie sits beside me and Rosie sits in front of us. He leans forward and rests his chin on the back of her seat. "Have you got a plan for tonight?"

"A plan?" She turns her head, and the sinking sun catches the curve of her cheek. Her fine, red hair is short and frizzy. "I plan to win."

Ossie laughs and reaches over to pat my knee. "Tara might have something to say about that!"

We all laugh, but I'm not finding the situation particularly funny. I suspect Rosie isn't either.

She changes the subject. "Are you still working at the nursery?"

"Yeah, the crazy time is done for now. Next big rush will be Christmas trees and holly wreaths."

Oh. *Nursery* as in place where people buy plants, not a place for looking after babies. Makes sense. Ossie may not be a big guy, but he's tanned and fit. The Celtic tattoo that wraps around his bicep is smooth and firm. Is it weird that I want to reach over and touch it? I smooth my skirt across my lap.

Ossie chats about organic vegetables. Bamboo. It's strange to listen to him talk about stuff that has nothing to do with poetry, nothing to do with Hannah.

Chapter Seventeen

A lot of familiar faces have come to Persephone's to see the big poetry showdown. There's an open mic first and then, instead of having a featured poet, Rosie and I will be the main course.

We'll each perform three poems, to be judged just like a regular slam.

Whoever gets more points will take the fourth spot on the team.

Ebony and Maddy show up just as the first open-mic reader is being introduced.

I can't listen properly. What should I perform? Should I do something old? Pre-Hannah?

When the open-mic readers are done, I whisper an apology in Rosie's ear. Then I head for the stage.

The monster who took the maiden
was lonely as dust
so lonely he would stop at nothing
to possess all of her.

Dark as a mountain
slicing into the soft belly of the sky
he followed her
watched as she stumbled.

The monster grew fat and happy
dining on rot wherever he found it—

compost bins, landfills, graveyards.
The maiden loved to fly
was once so alive she threw herself
against obstacles
off rooftops
knowing at the last moment
she would rise
soar in one great arc heavenward
land breathless and grinning on the
   other side
already charging forward.
No hesitation
no what-ifs
no but-I-can'ts
just a fast gallop over grass
aboard a blessed unicorn.

Until she crashed into a murky pool
where the monster lay waiting
a monster slippery as any
   water-dweller
hooked claws sank into damaged
   flesh

an embrace she was powerless to
  resist.
She knew he was there
but such was his power
she didn't run away
didn't invite him in
didn't have to.
He pushed his way inside
until he filled her
made her sway to the rhythm of his
    counting
      one two three four
      take that step
      and be no more.

The poem goes on to tell how the monster does terrible things to the maiden in his underwater cave. The lines *one two three four / take that step / and be no more* repeat several times. By the last one even I'm sick of it. The poem isn't good enough.

The judges agree. My scores aren't terrible, but they aren't great either. The average is around 7.6 or 7.7.

Rosie is up next and she gets the crowd right into her poem about the power of dessert. Even I have to laugh when she rolls her eyes and describes the ecstasy of diving into a chocolate layer cake. It's a crowd-pleaser for sure. Her lowest score is an 8.2.

Not a good start for me.

When I'm back on the stage, Ebony gives me a small nod of encouragement.

When the coffin drops the last few
   inches
the soft scrape of wood against dirt
tears a hole in the sky
and I am falling.
My aunt whispers, hold on hold on
as if this instruction can steady us all

stop my mother from
throwing herself in
after Hannah.

Wedged between my father my uncle
aunts grandmothers cousins
somehow I stand
anchored by the scent of lilies
heavy in my hands.

When you're ready
The uncle nudges me
not knowing I am blind
can't see the edge of the pit
through this sea of tears.

Every bad horror movie
I've ever seen
plays in the background
claws pushing aside dirt
black eyes, staring
what if she isn't in there?

what if she is, but isn't dead?
why, really, did they keep the casket
  closed?
Her dress ragged
her fists pounding, pounding
on the inside of the lid—
let me out let me out
let me come back, please.
I promise
I won't do it again.

All these people
pushing her back
shh, Hannah—you are at peace
  now—
shh, Hannah—your pain is done—
close your weary eyes
and...what?
enjoy your final resting place?

When the coffin drops the last few
  inches

the earth falls away beneath my feet
and I soar
like a black bird
swooping above
the heads bowed
with the weight of rules that say
when a child dies thou shalt be sad
when a child turns her back on you
forgive her.

My scores are a little better this time—all in the low 8s. Rosie's next poem is not nearly as funny as her first one. It's about how she learned to puke on demand. She talks fast and smooth, like someone selling fancy knives on TV. Her scores are pretty close to mine.

We take a short break after that. Rosie and I wind up beside each other in the hallway, waiting for the bathroom.

"Did you see this?" Rosie points at a flyer pinned to a notice board.

Suicide Survivors Support Group

"I used to go," she adds matter-of-factly.

The thought of being in a room full of people who have lost someone to suicide makes me shudder.

"I haven't been for a while. It was so…sad. And hard. But it was good too in a way—you know?"

I don't, but I nod anyway.

"It might be different—better—if I went with someone."

She can't seriously expect that I'll go with her?

The door opens to the bathroom and she slips inside. I think of her puking poem and wonder what she's doing in there. Do we never get to leave our pasts behind?

"Good luck," she says when she comes out.

"You too," I answer.

For my third poem I do "A Bus Rolls into the Shower Stall." The scores are good, but if Rosie has a strong finish, she'll win easily.

When it's Rosie's turn, it's obvious she's nervous, which isn't like her at all. Her hands quiver and she licks her lips several times before taking the microphone.

The day I jumped from the
*   Wishbone Bridge*
the sky was clear as a window to
*   heaven...*

Ossie reaches for my hand and squeezes it. I cannot tear my eyes from Rosie's face as she recites her poem. She is both radiant and terrified. Instead of her usual rapid-fire style, she delivers the opening lines in a slow, smooth roll of images. She stands on a bridge, silently apologizing to her family. She reminds herself why she is there, dizzy when she looks down at the water so far below.

Then she switches to a faster delivery and throws a string of abuse at herself, at us—

Fat worthless slug
ugly and useless
you deserve this and only this

Then she steps over the rail. Here Rosie slows down again and describes the moment of letting go, the moment when she teeters at the edge.

Is it too late
to reach for the railing
and pull myself to safety?
Falling. Falling.

Then there's the terrible moment when she realizes that she has just made an awful mistake. A mistake that's too late to fix.

I hold my breath and wait, wait, wait for the impact. Rosie slams into the water.

The bones in my feet shatter
ribs crack
my screams drown
in the siren's wail.

She delivers the final lines in a sweet, tender voice.

To be alive is to live with pain
knowing this, I'll never jump again.

When she comes back to the table I wrap her in a fierce hug. She doesn't pull away. We both burst into tears. All the hurt and grief and fury sobs out. She understands. I understand.

The organizer calls for a ten-minute break. It's just long enough for us to splash some cold water on our faces in the washroom.

"Ready?" I ask before we head back out into the bistro.

"Ready," Rosie says.

I have never cared less about the outcome of a slam. Rosie wins, which comes as no surprise to any of us. When I congratulate her, I mean it.

Nikki Tate is the bestselling author of more than twenty books for young readers. When she's not writing, storytelling or horseback riding, Nikki hosts a book club called "Titles and Tate" on CBC Radio's *All Points West*. She lives on Vancouver Island, British Columbia, with a varied menagerie of animals. Visit www.nikkitate.com for more information.

orca soundings

For more information on all the books
in the Orca Soundings series, please visit
www.orcabook.com.